Saying Good-bye from the Window

Saying Good-bye from the Window

Demetri H. Loupos

VANTAGE PRESS
New York

Illustrated by Tanya Stewart

FIRST EDITION

Published by Vantage Press, Inc.
419 Park Ave. South, New York, NY 10016

Manufactured in the United States of America
ISBN: 978-0-533-15704-4

Library of Congress Catalog Card No.: 2006911007

0 9 8 7 6 5 4 3 2 1

Saying Good-bye from the Window

When I was a child, our whole family would come together at my grandmother's house for all major events and holidays. Our greatest memories began and ended there. Her grandchildren, especially, always got a little extra from her unconditional love.

While us children would play together and have lots of fun, Grandmother would be in the kitchen cooking up the most delicious-smelling foods. Before she would send my parents, sister, and me on our way for the night, Grandmother would pack us a doggie bag filled with the delicious foods we had just eaten.

Then, she would smother us all with kisses and hugs as she walked us to the front door.

As she kissed me goodnight, she would always scratch my head with her fingers, tickling me.

As Grandmother did for all visitors leaving her home, she would then go to her front window and wave good-bye. I can still remember seeing her figure just behind the slightly drawn curtain, silhouetted by the streetlights and our car's headlights shining on her as we backed out of her driveway. My father would always smile and say, "Look at the little old lady saying good-bye from the window."

Our grandmother taught all of us how to be strong. Having lived most of her life as a widow, she lived her life devoted to making others, and most importantly her family, happy. She raised four children by herself. Never did she look at her own needs. She taught us all to endure hardship, how to never give up in life, and to thank God for every precious moment.

Years later, when I was in college, my father called and broke the sad news to me that she had fallen ill. I raced home from school to spend the last few days with her. I remember the harsh autumn winds pelting my car with leaves as I struggled to hold back the tears. I felt so cold and alone.

Grandmother could no longer speak, for she had suffered a major stroke. Late one night in the hospital as I sat alone praying by her bedside, she reached out with her hand and scratched my head lightly and tried to look at me. Now she couldn't wave good-bye to me, but was saying farewell in a different way. As she always did in life, she was again using her every last bit of strength to make others happy.

I smiled at her, embraced her, and told her, “Thank you, you have done well in your life, Grandma. We will always love you.” The next day she went up to heaven.

My uncle called and asked me to give the eulogy. I didn’t know what I was going to say. So, the night before her funeral, I drove to her home and pulled into her driveway.

I gazed up at her front window with the streetlights shining across the glass, and the leaves pelting my car in the strong autumn wind. But this time, the curtain was not drawn and the little old lady silhouetted in the streetlight was no longer there.

How I wished she would just appear again one last time.

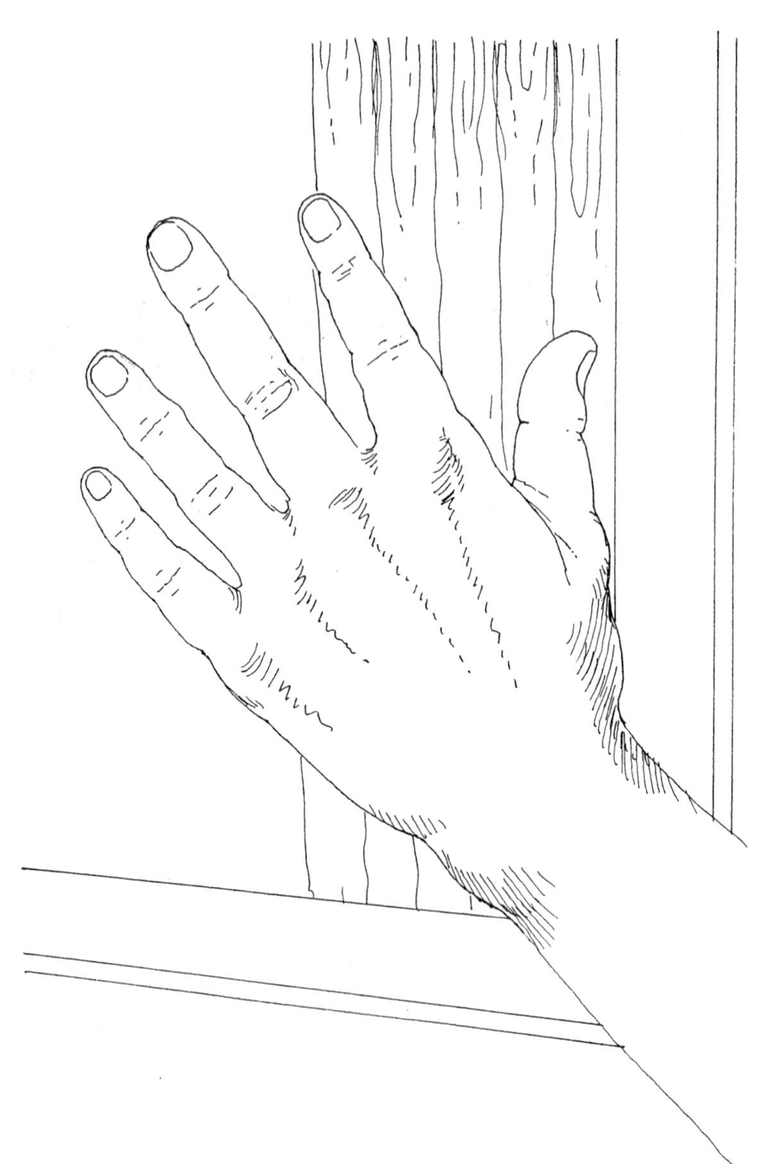

I even waved toward the window thinking she might somehow see me. But, she was gone forever. Again, I felt so cold and alone. But then my uncle showed up unexpectedly to check on her home. I tried to hide my tears.

"That's life, son," he said. And then we went inside her home and I stood in her front window. My uncle embraced me. It's amazing how our grandmother was still bringing us together as family.

I have since moved away, and Grandmother's house was eventually sold to new owners. I am sure the new family is now making many new windows.